IVOR

the engine
The Foxes

Story by OLIVER POSTGATE

Pictures by PETER FIRMIN

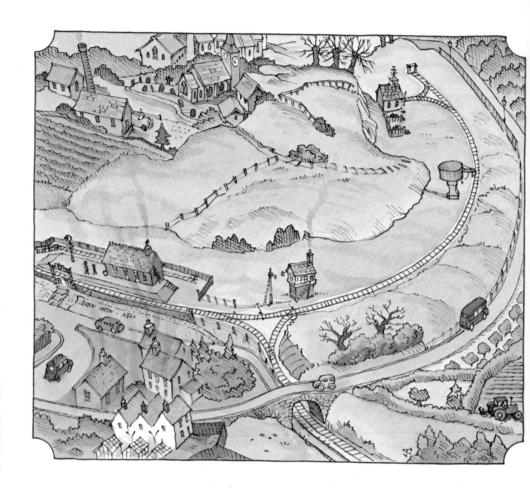

    Not very long ago, in the top left-hand
corner of Wales, there was a railway.
It wasn't a very long railway and it wasn't a
very important railway but it was called
The Merioneth and Llantisilly Rail Traction
Company Limited, and it was all there was.
    Beside a wood, beside some fields, beside
the railway stood the house of Mrs Porty.

It was a very posh house with a lovely garden and outside the garden gate, on the railway line, stood the Locomotive of the Merioneth and Llantisilly Rail Traction Company, whose name, as I am sure you have guessed, was Ivor the Engine.

Is that all?

No, where was Jones the Steam, Ivor's driver?

Jones the Steam and Mrs Porty were leaning on the fence looking into the overgrown wood near the house.

What were they looking at?

They were looking at foxes!

"There they are, Mr Jones!" cried Mrs Porty. "Three lovely foxcubs she has! Haven't you, Mrs Fox?"

The fox did not answer. I don't think she even heard Mrs Porty because Mrs Porty was whispering so as not to disturb her. In any case she was too busy looking proudly at her three fat cubs rolling and tumbling in the dust in front of their earth to take any notice of Jones and Mrs Porty.

"Oh, I hope the fox-hunters don't find them here!" sighed Mrs Porty. "They have been out rather a lot lately."

POOP POOP POOP! went Ivor's whistle.

"What is that for?" asked Mrs Porty.

"Oh, Ivor is keeping watch," explained Jones.

"From where he is standing he can see
Llaniog station. If any work cames in Dai
Station becomes very excited. He runs up and
down the platform shouting about engines
and engine-drivers not being where they
should be when they should be working!"

POOP POOPETY POOP!

"You'd better be off then, Jones," said Mrs Porty. "Oh, by the way, when you are down at the station, you might just see if my new hat has arrived. It's for the Institute Prize-giving tomorrow. It's a lovely hat, all high with feathers and a sort of . . ."

"Er, yes, well I will go and see if it is there,"
said Jones. "You look after the cubs now,
Mrs Fox, and you look after the foxes now,
Mrs Porty."

POOP! CHUFF . . . CHUFF . . . CHUFF . . .
Jones swung into Ivor's cab and they rolled
down towards Llaniog Station.

Dai Station stopped running up and down
when he saw them. He was looking very cross.
"Oh, there you are at last!" he said,
"Where have you been? This hatbox has come
for Mrs Porty . . . Very Urgent it says, deliver
immediately. Handle with great care!"
"Oh yes, it's a lovely hat," said Jones.
"All feathers and high, with a veil and . . ."

"I daresay," interrupted Dai, "but your job
is to deliver it, not talk about it. You had
better take it up to Mrs Porty right away, or
she'll be on the telephone shouting for it!"

"Mrs Porty does not shout," said Jones.
"As a matter of fact we were up there just now.
The fox in her wood has had three lovely cubs."

"Oh, nature-study is it?" growled Dai.

"You had better watch out! If Head Office came to hear of it, you'd be in trouble, taking time off to watch foxes indeed! And the foxes had better watch out too! The hunt is about today."

"Oh, don't speak of it, Dai!" sighed Jones.

"Speak of it!" said Dai, "I can hear them!"

They listened.

Tarroo Tarrooo!

They heard the distant sound of the huntsman's horn and the baying of the hounds.

"Oh Dai, I can hear them!" shouted Jones,
"What shall I do?"

"Climb on the roof!" suggested Dai.

Jones was puzzled. "What on earth for?
They are not hunting me. They hunt foxes."

"No, silly," said Dai. "Climb up so that you
can see where they are! Quick, I'll give you a
bunk up."

Jones clambered on to the roof and held on
to the chimney pot.

"I can see them!" he shouted. They are heading across Pugh's field towards Mrs Porty's wood."

"Isn't that where the foxes are?" Dai.

"Yes! And they are heading straight towards them!"

"Oh dear!"

"There's Mrs Fox now! I can see her!
She has left the wood and she is running
away over the field."

"Why is she doing that?"

"I expect she is leading the hunt away from
her cubs." shouted Jones.

"Which way is she going?"

"Down towards the bridge."

POOOOOP! went Ivor's whistle.

"Yes!" shouted Jones, as he jumped down.

"And don't forget Mrs Porty's hat!" added
Dai, pitching the pretty hatbox into Ivor's cab
as he began to move.

CHUFF...CHUFF...CHUFF...CHUFF.

Jones and Ivor sped down the line as fast as
his wheels would go.

"*Tarroo taroo!*" The hunt, a pack of baying hounds, followed by handsome horses ridden by ladies and gentlemen in scarlet coats, was streaming across the fields, and far ahead of them, Mrs Fox was streaking like a red flash across the grass.

"Stop by the bridge, Ivor!" shouted Jones.
The fox was running beside the stream as
Ivor slapped on his brakes by the bridge.

"She has seen us. Be ready!" whispered Jones.
The fox swerved and ran up the bank
towards them.

"NOW!" shouted Jones.
    PSSSSSSSSSSSSTT.
    The fox vanished into a vast cloud of steam which engulfed Ivor and Jones and the bridge.
    The hounds ran into the steam. The horses ran into the steam. But nobody could do anything until the steam cleared a bit.

"I say, Railwayman," said the huntsman, wiping his streaming eyes. "Do you have to make so much steam like that? It's a bit inconvenient for us, don't you know?"

"Oh, I was just blowing out the pipes a bit," said Jones. "We have to do it now and then . . . like sneezing, you know."

"I say, Railwayman," said the huntsman, "what on earth is that on your head?"

"Oh, the hat? That's for the Institute Prize-giving tomorrow. It's a lovely hat, look, all high, with feathers and a veil and . . ."

"Oh well, I daresay it's a very charming hat, Old Boy, but what we are looking for is a fox. You know, a fox!"

"Oh, I know, a fox," agreed Jones.

"Well, have you seen one, dammit?" barked the huntsman.

"Yes, I did happen to see one," said Jones, "but I don't think she wanted to see you . . . do you, Ivor?"

POOP POOPETY POOP POOP! laughed Ivor.

"Good day to you, Gentlemen!" said Jones.
CHUFF CHUFF CHUFF CHUFF . . .
The huntsmen watched Ivor move away.
Jones waved to them and the dirty feathers
on his hat flapped about in the wind.

"What an extraordinary chap!" said the
huntsman.

"Oh, come along Carruthers," said another

huntsman, "we must find that fox."

They did not find that fox. They searched all around the bridge, but there was no trace of it anywhere.

Meanwhile, Jones and Ivor came down to the points behind the Post Office at Llaniog.

Mrs Williams the Postmistress threw open her window.

"Oh Mr Jones! It really suits you!" she cried.

"Yes, it's a lovely hat, look," said Jones, "all high, with feathers and a . . ."

"I can see that!" said Mrs Williams. "It's a lovely hat, but it isn't yours, is it?"

"Oh no, it's for Mrs Porty," said Jones.

"Why are you wearing it, then?"

"Oh, you'd only laugh if I told you," said
Jones as he opened the regulator.

POOP POOP CHUFF CHUFF CHUFF...
they moved away up the line.

"I'll bet Mrs Porty won't laugh when she
sees her new hat," said Mrs Williams as she
closed her window.

She was quite right about that.

Mrs Porty saw Jones the Steam come up the path carrying the hatbox and she met him on the front porch with a face like a thundercloud.

"Mr Jones!" she roared, "you are wearing my hat!"

Jones looked very worried.

"Now wait a minute, Mrs Porty," he

stammered, "wait while I tell you what happened."

"Where is your own hat, Mr Jones?"

"Oh, mine is in the hatbox, it doesn't spoil so easily you see . . ."

"Spoil!" roared Mrs Porty, glaring at the grimy windblown feathers on Jones's head, "that hat is completely spoiled already!"

"Well, it was the hunt, you see," explained Jones. "And there was nowhere else she could go and . . . wait a minute . . ."

Mrs Porty glowered, while Jones undid the ribbon on the hatbox.

Out leaped a cloud of tissue paper, Jones's old blue cap and a streak of red fur.

"Mrs Fox!" shouted Mrs Porty.

Mrs Fox shot across the garden and dived
into the wood with her cubs.

"Yes, you see, I thought you would rather,"
stammered Jones.

Mrs Porty smiled: "Oh yes, I do see, yes, and
I certainly would rather, yes, of course, I am
glad you did . . . and the hat . . ."

Jones took off the hat and gave it to her.

"Yes," said Mrs Porty, "I am sure that it will be perfectly all right with a bit of tidying up!"

And it was. The hat looked lovely at the Institute Prize-giving the next day . . . a bit blackish about the feathers, but quite lovely!

This edition published 1994 by Diamond Books
77-85 Fulham Palace Road, Hammersmith London W6 8JB

First published by Picture Lions 1979
14 St James's Place, London SW1

Printed in Slovenia

ISBN 0 261 66573-1